ALL FOR A BUCK

Doris Anne Beaulieu

DEDICATION

I dedicate the findings of how life was for these very young men after being drafted into the Vietnam War, and what they faced upon returning home, to my fellow advocate and friend who shared his many stories of the treatment he received the minute he stepped off the bus—returning home from hell.

He also told stories of all he and his family endured because the military lost his records, which they claimed had been destroyed in a fire—after everything he had already gone through.

He shared these stories in detail during our many trips to Augusta, where we were part of a statewide low-income group called the

"Maine Association of Independent Neighborhoods," where I served as Vice President. Together, we worked on many legislative issues to help our communities. Mainers might remember seeing me on the eleven o'clock news the night President Ronald Reagan was shot at—I was testifying at the State House on some of Maine's low-income housing issues. By the way, we won—and laws were changed.

I felt compelled to write a story that would bring some of these issues to light. I hope this story allows you to understand what life was truly like for these veterans, from their point of view, and helps set the historical record straight.

CONTENTS

Senior Year … 1

The Draft … 7

Jobs After War … 11

Who Is It? … 20

Expanding The Search … 28

The Clue To Who? … 34

Arrest … 42

Court Date … 50

Do They Have Their Man? … 60

Finally Have A Case … 70

Finding Their Way … 75

CHAPTER I

Senior Year

Senior year of high school had finally arrived for three best friends. Just one more year to go before they could start their future plans. They had been working the past few summers, saving *all* their money to go into business together after graduation.

Sam's summer job was working as a mechanic. He enjoyed working with his hands and addressing people's needs. He had just married Sue, who was also a people person, working in an insurance agency. She supported her husband's plans with his lifelong friends as she worked to learn all she could about filing claims.

Mike was a book-smart, brainy type of person. Making money work for him was his greatest skill. He could always stretch a dollar or make deals and come out smiling. He had been studying the business world for as long as anyone could remember—always learning what was working and what was failing—which excited his friends. They looked at Mike as the man with the business head. He had a girlfriend, Liz, who worked in a beauty salon. She was very excited for Mike and his plans, and she knew he had the brains to write his own ticket in life. They hoped to marry after Mike and his friends got their business off the ground.

Kevin was an organizer. He would date, but had no steady girlfriend. He believed he should have a home first and enough money to support a wife before looking for something long-lasting. He had planned that part of his life out years ago and hadn't changed a thing since. His summer job was working in a furniture showroom— organizing displays and creating a comfortable, welcoming space. He wanted to show that if you set up all the pieces to a room in a way that's inviting, customers were more likely to buy the whole room. His way of doing things brought more sales to the store, and they loved his touch—designing rooms differently every week. It made for great pictures in the papers for ads. People would look in from the storefront window and feel such warmth from the setup that they'd end up inside, and with the store's payment plan, they could have it just as it was displayed.

Senior year was well on its way. The "A" Team, they called themselves, were planning to go into the car dealership business. Mike was already working on proposals for banks and car companies. Knowing what to sell in the area—based on average wages—was key to figuring out which vehicles people would go for first.

The guys met every Saturday night to talk about what each had done and what the next step was for everyone. Mike discussed his proposals and asked for input on who they should approach first, as they were all equal partners.

Sam checked out places for their dealership, contacting only buildings off the main roads. He made appointments to check the places out in order to see if they fit the mechanical needs and what they had to supply, such as working lifts, benches, and so on.

Mike was collecting the information needed to figure out an estimated cost to start up and the running costs, while Kevin organized a list of what was needed.

By the time Thanksgiving came around, they had so much to celebrate with their friends, family, and the public. They had their building locked down. The banks were in favor and finalizing the paperwork. Kevin had advertising ads ready to go and banners for the grand opening day. Sam had collected tools needed for three mechanics so far. A few top mechanics from the high school shop had already approached Sam for a job. Kevin had salesmen ready, with three positions to be filled after graduation.

A big banquet was set, with their three families footing the bill. The newspapers and local TV stations were covering the celebration as a Thanksgiving dinner for all they had to be thankful for. The article was a lesson to the young—that they too could succeed in business at their young age, fresh out of high school. Everyone was congratulating them on the street, and many were asking for a job. They were running high and knew they had made a lot of upcoming customers. Every conversation became a sales pitch. They had very supportive, proud parents on their side as they moved on, doing all they could until graduation day.

CHAPTER II

The Draft

On December 1st, their lives and future plans were pulled right from under their feet. They were drafted into the Vietnam War and had to report immediately. Sam had just found out Sue was pregnant and didn't know if he'd ever see his child. Their planned future, and all the money poured into it, was going down the drain. Sam was to report to the Navy. He felt it was due to his mechanical skills.

Mike had to report to the Army—he was more into leadership material—and Kevin to the Air Force. The reason was unclear, but he felt it was because he paid close attention to detail.

Maybe none of those details mattered. In those days, you were just a number and a body to the government. Their number had just come up. Could be more for the fact that 805 people sent from their town were from poor, working-class families. They tended to go for less-educated men who had not yet graduated. That could have been the key, since they were barely 18. There were a few who were exempt from the draft, but not these three men. You had no choice—be drafted or be a draft offender and be convicted and jailed.

They had seen so much and were forced to be part of horrible, unbelievable situations. Their view of the world changed forever. Many had turned to drugs or alcohol to deal with the overwhelming emotions from the horror they faced every second of the day, just to keep moving. The biggest thought was why their government put them into that situation with no choice of their own. *Why?*

Those who made it home came back with injuries inside and out—and things only got worse. They went from war to civilian life in only two days. Disappointment and abandonment hit real hard the minute they got off the bus. They were greeted by crowds filled with hostility, spitting at them, calling them murderers and baby killers. All causing more emotional problems than they already carried, adding to the nightmares.

Family and what used to be friends acted uncomfortable around them, as if to say, stay away from us. The government uprooted their lives, and they got no appreciation or support for serving their country.

Adapting to civilian life felt more like having to isolate oneself. Help from the VA was difficult, as records ended up lost. This fact created angry outbursts in vets and paranoia. Finding a job was difficult, to say the least. Who would hire them, with all the hostility toward them in the community? They needed jobs away from people—and they knew it—for the safety of others and themselves.

CHAPTER III

Jobs After War

Mike had it the worst, being in the Army. He had seen more and lost more—men who became more than friends, more like lifesavers. The Army lost 38,209 men. The Marines lost 14,838. The Air Force lost 2,584. The Navy lost 2,555 and seven Coast Guardsmen were lost. Most men were the age of 20.

Returning to civilian life was full of flashbacks and nightmares. His girlfriend Liz stood by him and all that now came with it. They married at home with only their parents and siblings—no newspaper announcement. Mike became a lumberjack, working alone in the peacefulness of the woods. This helped him calm down and stay busy. He slowly learned to adjust to civilian life by putting distance between people and himself. It was good for his soul and helped him find his inner self to feel whole again.

The wood market was booming as men returned from war. Their return created the need for more housing, as comfort within a family was best for these vets. An increase in childbirth caused a greater need for farmland and housing. Apartment life was not suited for these vets' lives or protection. They needed space between themselves and neighbors to properly have time to re-adjust to civilian life on their own terms.

Sam, who had gotten married to Sue before the draft, went to work in the wood mill. He used his mechanical skills to run the pulp side of the mill, which turns wood into paper or cardboard. This meant fewer people to deal with, as teams were only three to four people who were very aware of his medication. Sue and Sam were adding to their family size, so a good-paying job with insurance was a must.

Kevin worked in the wood yard of the same mill, pretty much by himself, running a loader with a grapple to pick logs, mostly going to the chipper. Between his war money and the great-paying job he now had, his house was almost fixed up and paid off. His difficulties adapting to civilian life still made him uncomfortable being around people, which hindered him from working on a personal relationship. He told himself he still needed to follow his goals of having a home before a lady and hoped time would handle the rest.

They were the lucky ones who were able to find jobs when they returned home after the war. Somehow, the war within themselves was one of readjusting and overcoming what they had seen and done to be able to return home. The screams of their comrades as they were tortured to death were always on their minds when night time came—as well as the faces of many children being used in this war.

Something that time can never take away.

Keeping busy and focusing on the task at hand was the best way to let time soften the emotional wounds of the war our government pushed young men into. The three men were polite to each other in public but feared any gathering, as it would just turn into talking about the war they wished to leave behind. Their once dream of running that well-planned business together had passed its time.

As life continued, Mike and Liz were on their second child. They would picnic in the woods on sunny summer days. When the skidder stopped for lunch, the children knew it was time to run wild and see what they could find for crafts in the afternoon while Dad continued to work. Mom always brought craft supplies to keep the children busy. Things like double acorns, funny-looking pinecones, and bird feathers were always part of the find. They got to see deer and wild rabbits—though Mom always had to say they couldn't take them home because they belonged to nature; they were not pets. Spotting the first fawn became a game on every visit to the woods where Dad worked.

In mid-afternoon, depending on the season, it was time to pick raspberries or apples. With pies for supper the next day for sure. Some raspberries went into winter jam, and apples into applesauce for winter needs. Canning was a big part of country life to prepare for the months when work was not so plentiful. The woods also provided them with their winter meat during hunting season. Deer steak on the cast-iron skillet was most of their winter meat and went well with mashed potatoes. On top of all the vegetables from the garden that were canned and the potatoes they picked when school started.

Sam and Sue were also adding to their family. They were on number four, and all boys. Sam did not have a chance to save his war money since he had already been married to Sue, and she was pregnant right before the draft. Money was hard for them, and every penny saved was highly needed. Sam took part in every meat sport season, and his right-on aim got him attention in the military. He would take his all boys fishing and made their mom proud every time they came home with their limit. Only the first son was old enough for turkey and deer hunting. They both would get their deer with or without help, as the meat was needed. After all, they now were a family of six to feed.

Kevin got his house paid for. Now it was time to turn his house into a home and have a family of his own. It would have to be a woman who understood what he went through. His anxiety and PTSD always seemed to act up when he tried to talk to a lady. Starting a conversation about being to war was a fear he added to himself. The hostility and name-calling he endured the minute he got off the bus when he returned home caused him severe anxiety. The VA lost all of his medical records, which stopped him from getting the proper care he truly needed. Many Vietnam veterans felt their records were destroyed or missing because it was at the time looked at as a war we did not belong in, so help should not be given. Even though they got drafted by their own government to serve their country.

One day in the park, a lady sat by Kevin. Her name was Belinda. She was at the park with her two children, watching them play, a boy and a girl. As they played, she began to talk to Kevin about her struggles of raising two kids alone. She stated she had lost her husband in the war and had no family support due to the public image surrounding the Vietnam War. Kevin felt more at ease the more she talked about how her community was treating her—kind of like something about the war had rubbed off on her personally. Kevin finally told her he was one of those vets. He was at peace with himself at her reaction, and for once in four years of being home, he didn't feel alone. Kevin and Belinda were married by late October and were working on having a child.

CHAPTER IV

Who Is It?

Kevin was doing well at work, and with his house paid off, he had Belinda start college funds for her two previous children using the benefits they were receiving under their father—to set them up in life down the road. Hunting season had come upon them, and Kevin used it as his relaxing time in the woods, like he used to do with his dad growing up. Kevin continued the old routine and hoped one day to do the same with a child of his own. It was a quiet time, surrounded by peacefulness as you sit, wait, and reflect on your life—listening to the birds wake up in the morning and the first sounds of animals moving.

This year, Kevin only wanted to get that trophy buck for the living room wall. He wanted the kids to be proud of him, and he needed the meat too, with a family now to support. Opening day led to only does, but he knew those does would bring him a buck in the days to come. Rut season was about to take place, and he knew where to be early in the morning for that. He had put up deer cameras to track their usual travel across his property.

As he worked the next week in the mill's wood yard, he was thinking about where he would sit come Saturday for the 14-point buck he had seen on his deer cam. His job of cutting logs eight feet long for the debarking and then the chipper had become routine, which gave Kevin plenty of time to reflect on his own thoughts. Lunchtime came, and he had a good pill to keep things running through his half-hour break.

As Kevin made his way back after lunch to the wood yard, he walked by the chipper and saw red all over the chips—and pieces of flesh everywhere. Flashbacks and paranoia hit full force, and in an angry outburst, half out of air, he ran to the office. An alarm came on, and over the intercom, they said all shift leaders needed to count their people so everyone could be accounted for. The mill began shutting down, and police entered the building. No one was allowed in or out of the mill, even after their shift, until the investigation was complete.

Shutting down a mill that size, which runs 24/7, was a loss of millions of dollars. However, it had to be done, and the ringing of alarms was unbelievable. It would take a day for each department to shut down, step by step, taking their turns—all done by department in the order of the process.

Kevin and Sam did find each other. After all they had been through in the war, they were glad to see each other and knew Mike being in the woods was alright. The mill had over a thousand workers, so it was past midnight before they were allowed to go home. Kevin was the only one ordered by police and investigators to return in the morning for more questioning.

Over a thousand people would be at the unemployment line in the morning, as pink slips were passed out as they left for the night. No one knew how long they would be out of work—or if the job would still be there. Who was it? Or was there more than one person? How did they get in if everyone was accounted for?

Kevin arrived at nine as told and was questioned by many agencies, all asking the same questions. This caused his PTSD to flare up, which only made things worse for him when they realized he was a Vietnam vet. He became their prime suspect at that point— just no clear evidence to arrest him yet.

The mill spent the rest of the week calling every employee personally, even though the headcount had everyone accounted for. Many people had traded shifts for personal reasons with one another, so this was one more step to make sure no employee was missing.

All seemed to be accounted for, as the public watched the news for more updates. Employees were not happy with their unemployment checks, which were half of what they had been making and put a cramp in the lifestyle they were used to. Cutting back was a must, as some tried to find other jobs that paid more than the unemployment check. But no one was willing to hire them, as most felt it was temporary and the mill would be up and running soon.

All pulp drivers for the mill were put on hold, and they were checking them all out to make sure no one was missing, even though all pulp trucks were gone from the yard. Anyone who delivered to the mill had all their personal records checked out.

Now they turned their attention to the process of what happens after the logs get delivered, to see how anyone could have gotten through to put a body in after making it into the gated area, with guards on duty the whole time. Checking the logbook, someone was on duty at all times. They called the guards in and questioned them, and all had been done correctly.

After the logs were cut into eight-foot lengths, they got fed into the chipper that makes two different piles: one of softwood and one of hardwood. A bulldozer spreads each pile out to make room for more. This is a continuous process and gets mixed only at the next stage by weight, to create what the mill at the time is making—mostly paper or cardboard, and at times, specialty paper.

They found the blood to be only one type, so that told them only one person had been killed. So far, this process of elimination is in its fourth week, and the public is feeling very unsafe walking the streets at night. The public is now at the point of protesting—most from those who want to return to work in order to continue the lifestyle that was taken from them. Others feel those protesting are self-centered and not caring about the life that was

taken. Opposite sides in a protest are never
good.

CHAPTER V

Expanding the Search

All security cameras were being looked at again with a fine-tooth comb to see if someone had gotten through the gates or come from a worker's vehicle in the parking lot. They also checked to see if anyone was in an area where they didn't belong. They knew it was a lost cause but needed to check it out again anyhow. However, they did discover some blind spots where no cameras were installed, although the mill used cameras mostly to watch workers for safety while they worked.

The log deliveries had their own entrance to the mill, so a more detailed background check on pulp drivers and the workers from the wood yards where the logs came from was needed. They had to call in to find out if the blood was male or female, just to see if this could have been a lovers' spat. It turned out to be male, so the idea of a driver having a fling gone wrong was taken off the table. Now came the thought that it might have been a woman caught by her husband, and a fight took place between two men. Maybe an accident happened during the fight, and the body needed to be disposed of.

The investigation was going nowhere, with more questions left unanswered. The mill was losing millions a day with no work getting done. The bills were piling up with no end in sight. Many workers moved to fill jobs at other mills within the state. Only five mills were left in the state, and even though some found work, it still left about 800 people without jobs in the area.

The mill decided, once given the okay, to proceed with their annual shutdown for cleanup and repairs. With a skeleton crew, they began. Investigators were overseeing every part of the cleaning and repairs—something the mill did not take into consideration when they decided to use the downtime. It was a cost not anticipated but understood, as nothing had been found yet to identify the person whose life was lost in the chipper.

The outcry from the community had grown. No one had faith in the investigators' ability to do their jobs. Workers were at the point of losing things they could no longer afford on such small unemployment checks they were receiving. Rumors of the mill closing had put a heavy burden on the investigators to find some kind of clue somewhere. Workers were now fighting to get into the mill to do their own investigation. Many who were known to be calm workers found themselves arrested for trying to get into the mill to do the investigators' jobs for them.

After three months, people were losing what they owned. They decided to ask a top person—called a P1—who knew every step of the mill, to explain the process while doing a walk-through from beginning to end. He stated where the logs got delivered, and for the twentieth time or more, they found nothing. They entered the area of the chipper, knowing all power had been turned off. The only things they had found were some loose change and a wedding band. Both bins of softwood and hardwood had been mixed due to investigators going through them while checking for clues.

The head guy explained the importance of why the two bins were kept separate and only mixed by weight on the conveyor belt according to the product they were making to fill an order. It's then fed to the digester.

The guy suddenly rushed off, and the investigators tried to stop him. When they finally grabbed him and got him to the floor, the head guy hollered, "Alarm!" The investigators pulled him to his feet. The alarm had gone off as they were shutting the mill down.

"So what does that mean?" one of the investigators asked.

After the chips are weighed, the belt feeds down to the digester, which has magnets mounted above. If any form of metal is picked up, the alarm goes off, and the belt is stopped.

"That's the alarm we heard while shutting down this department," the man said. "We need to go see what's on the magnet."

The investigators let go of him and followed.

CHAPTER VI

The Clue to Who?

They get to the magnet and discover a set of keys stuck to it. First, they work on getting an electrician there to make sure everything is disconnected, so the machine doesn't accidentally start—since a man needs to go in and push all the chips through. If nothing turns up, the entire inside of the machine will need a closer inspection. There's about a 400-foot belt of chips to check. It's now been a good four months since the mill was shut down. Along with added costs for whatever the investigators need—insurance, taxes, and loss of workforce—the mill has now decided to permanently shut down.

Another week passes as they continue to check and recheck the chips on the belt. Finally, the investigators catch a break. They find a badge belonging to a game warden. At first, the question is: what does a game warden have to do with the mill? Secondly, how did he end up here? The head guy—who is a P1—says nothing, and there's no record on the guard logs of a game warden having permission to be in the mill for any reason. Everyone has to check in at the gate, and anyone in question is escorted to the office.

Was this a mill worker getting rid of a body? Nothing showed up on the cameras, and a body is pretty hard to hide—even with the blind spots the investigators had pointed out. Still, there's no clear explanation for how a person could have made it to the chipper with a body.

To the investigator, this suggests the person was dead before ending up in the chipper. There's some comfort in that—but still, a person is dead. Seeing that there are still chips on the digest belt, the investigators want the rest of them checked for any more possible clues. They find a bullet, damaged by the chipper, which indicates the warden had been shot.

The next step is to call the state warden office to find out if anyone is missing. Sure enough, they are—but they had never thought to connect their missing man with what was happening at the mill. They take the mutilated badge and keys to confirm it was their man.

The wardens now join the investigation team, determined to find out how this all happened. First, they begin looking into the warden's activities during the days leading up to his disappearance. For these investigators, it's not just about the day he went missing—but how he ended up at the mill at all.

First, it was made clear to the investigators that this warden would sometimes go off course, as things could happen while heading toward his reported assignments. However, it was usually still within the same general area, and this warden had a very good track record for issuing fines.

The public was told who the warden was that had been connected to the mill accident. Many laid-off workers were hopeful this revelation would change the mind of the mill owner and lead to reopening the mill. However, it seemed the bills had added up too high, and the costs associated with the death caused the insurance company to drop them. That didn't seem fair to the unemployed workers, as the warden wasn't killed by the mill but became a victim *at* the mill. Surely, they thought, that could be fought in court—and won.

This warden had caught many poachers over the years while on his way to question people suspected of breaking the law, and he had won several awards for his work. He'd been with the warden service for twelve years. So finding out who did this to him—and why—was very important, not only to the warden service but also to the public, who knew him and counted on him to keep them safe during hunting season.

Records showed that he had called for backup, but when help arrived, nothing was found—not even his truck. They believed he was on foot, as no blood was found at the scene. They did find deer blood and guts, which was normal for that time of year. Samples were taken, but so far nothing matched any of the deer meat they tested. Investigators initially saw it as a hunting accident gone wrong.

A farmer down the road was the last person to speak with the warden, and that was the area where they believed he had been when he disappeared that morning. It was about a half hour before the call for backup came in. This time of year is always tough on wardens, with so many calls that they can't always go in pairs—and this was one of those times. The farmer had told the warden that three guys were crossing his field hunting together. That's the same thing he told investigators when he called for help. The farmer had been nervous because the men were hiding in his cornfield, too close to the house, and he had watched them from the milking parlor window.

The investigators for the mill decided to go talk to the farmer themselves. One major takeaway from their conversation was that he does not confront people crossing his field and always calls it in. He also seemed agitated with the Vietnam vet who was working the woodlot on the land next to his farm.

The farmer explained that one of his cows got loose and wandered onto the woodlot to the right of his property, and he had to call the cops to help retrieve the cow and stay until he could fix the fence. He stated that the lot wasn't even his—he was only the cutter. He went on to say that those vets "aren't right in the head," claiming the man next door had anxiety problems and warning them to be careful when talking to him. He also mentioned that the man keeps a rifle in the back window of his truck.

The investigators called the police to verify the farmer's story and confirmed that it was true and had indeed happened. The police report also listed the man's name as Mike, a Vietnam vet in need of help readjusting to civilian life.

CHAPTER VII

Arrest

At first, Mike keeps working until they're very close to him. He stops sawing and asks, "What do you want? Make it fast!" They ask him if he saw a game warden around during hunting season.

Mike responds, "Am I looking at some now?"

They ask, "Have you had any trouble around here, like with hunters?"

Mike states, "Why would hunters come around here with all this noise from the saw and skidder constantly going? It's enough to scare all the animals away. The only problem is that kook of a farmer who thinks I need to stop working so his getaway cow can hold still long enough for him to catch it. Did you know he called the cops on me 'cause I didn't help him get his cow? He somehow knew I was a Vietnam vet and called me a baby killer. There's no way I was going to help him do shit.

"Now I need to get back to work—I have a family to support and a truck coming for my logs that I need to get up by the road for pick-up. So go help the kook catch his cows."

"This is not about a cow, Mike," one investigator says. "It's about a man who got put through the chipper at the mill where your logs end up."

Mike replies, "What? I don't even know which mill these logs end up at. There's a big difference between a log and a person. And they think I need help? Get out of here!"

The investigators leave and agree Mike has a point, and they understand the problem with the farmer. It's obvious the farmer has a problem with Vietnam vets, which may be because he himself is a vet from a different war—one that wasn't looked down on the same way.

The investigators continue talking to people in the area about shots being fired during hunting season, going house to house. They get to an elderly man's house who claims he called a game warden about gunfire that hit his house. When he showed them the card he kept, it was from the game warden who got killed. They finally had a lead and felt like they were getting somewhere. The old man had called the warden directly—not the station—so the call was never recorded.

He told the investigators that his neighbor down the road got laid off from the mill and hasn't been able to find a new job. He stated, "Unemployment, you know, doesn't add up to what he was making at the mill. Anyhow, unemployment was giving him a hard time because of the quarter you have to meet to qualify, and he was new to the mill. They told him to go get help from the VA, but they can't find any records of him—even that he went to war.

"He has a family to feed, so he hunts a lot. His wife goes to the food bank weekly, but I don't think he knows that. I know because I volunteer there. I feel bad for them. It's sad how they're treated by their own community.

"Before the draft, he was one of three boys who were the town heroes. Had their lives all planned out after graduation, and everyone looked up to them as examples for our youth.

I just wanted the warden to talk to Sam about the law stating how far you have to be from a person's home to shoot. I wasn't making a formal complaint or anything. I'm not totally sure it was him, but I do see him hunt the area for every hunting sport there is."

The investigators are now joined by a warden as they go to Sam's house. They feel this must be their man. Sam was cleaning his guns when the officers arrived. They noticed a pile of deer skins as they walked by the garage, where a side door was partly open, on their way to the main entrance of the house.

As Sam opens the door, the officers—who have now taken over the case—notice guns on the table and ask Sam to please step outside.

Sam replies, "No. This is my home. I'm busy, so you can come in or leave."

The wardens look at each other and decide to enter. Sam continues cleaning his guns.

The wardens ask, "What are you doing?"

Sam asks the one who questioned him, "Are you a vet?"

"Yes," the warden replies.

"Did they lose your records?"

The same warden replies, "No."

"Go get yourself some help if you can't see what I'm doing."

"You've been shooting a lot lately," one says.

"Of course. I bought this place because of the wildlife, and I go shooting a good part of the year—whatever season it is."

"Sam was looking down the barrel to see if more cleaning was needed when the officers asked, "Shot any game wardens lately?"

Sam was shocked at the question and lifted the gun a bit at that moment. The officers grabbed his gun and handcuffed him.

"We're taking you in for questioning," one says, and they seize all his guns.

A warrant is sought from the court to search the home. The bullet found on the chipper belt was a .30-30, coming from a lever-action gun. The bullet was damaged by the chipper, so an exact match could not be determined. However, they had Sam on record as working at the mill and, in the past, being accused of poaching—though the charges were dropped.

Sam did own a .30-30 Winchester, and nine deer furs were collected from the garage. Sam kept his mouth shut at the police station, like he'd learned to do during the war. The whole time, he was thinking. His one phone call was to Kevin.

Kevin worked in the woodyard at the mill, but his job was to cut the logs into eight-foot sections and feed them to the chipper. Luckily for him, he lived two towns over from the area where the warden had been assigned.

CHAPTER VIII

Court Date

Kevin had called Mike to pick his brain after Sam's one phone call from the police station, where he was able to collect the court date from Sam. Mike informed Kevin about his run-in with the officers and the neighbor's cow. So, Mike was clearly all in to help his lifelong friend Sam.

The wardens did not know Mike, so he sat in the back of the courtroom waiting for the right moment. The wardens presented their case: the elderly neighbor claimed shots were always being fired on Sam's property, and that a bullet had hit his house. Sam was cleaning guns when they arrived and had pointed one at them. They also mentioned the nine deer furs in Sam's garage. He had been laid off at the mill, wasn't receiving unemployment benefits, and the military had no record of him ever serving. Meat in his freezer was from several different deer. Their most important claim was that he worked at the mill on the first step that fed the logs into the chipper—which led to the conveyor belt to the digester feed belt—where they found the warden's key, bullet, and badge.

Kevin had handed Sam a folder when he first entered the courtroom, and Sam was looking it over as the wardens spoke, trying to make their case. The wardens were not expecting outside help and thought this was an open-and-shut case—they wanted a win to ease the public.

Then it was Sam's turn to speak.

"Your Honor, I'm a Vietnam vet, and I get discriminated against a lot because of that—often with hatred. That might be why I'm having trouble collecting unemployment from the mill. I only worked there for six months, but it's something about how the quarters worked. I did provide my pay stubs and my bank records to prove I served my country. So I *do* have a service record, and here are copies of both.

If the wardens had taken the time to check my maple syrup smokehouse up the hill, they would have found many more deer furs and beaver pelts. I have two bins there where people can drop them off—folks who don't want to be seen publicly but understand my Vietnam vet situation. I'm just grateful for the support.

I sell the fur to cover the cost of my electric bill. As for the meat in my freezer—people know my situation, and when they hunt on my property, they give me meat as thanks for letting them hunt. Again, I'm grateful. It helps me feed my family.

I did not hit the old man's house. He stated he didn't see who did it and just assumed it was me. Clearly, I wouldn't do that—and my neighbor and I get along just fine."

Sam turns and motions to Mike, who opens the courtroom doors for some 30-plus people to walk in and tell the judge how they helped Sam support his family. They gave testimonies about tagging their deer and the meat they gave Sam in appreciation for letting them and their sons hunt his property. The officers had to sit there and listen to it all.

Then Sam tells the judge that before he got drafted, he and a few buddies were about to start a car dealership after graduation, and he was going to be the mechanic of the place. He handed the judge a ledger of vehicle repairs done—the whole week in question was filled with work that got done and paid the mortgage on his house. He proceeded to tell the judge those witnesses who visited during their repairs were here to testify. The judge listened to those from the day the warden went missing and hit his gavel hard. Case dismissed.

The officers were back to square one. They knew someone they had already talked to was guilty of murder. They broke up into groups of two to hide and watch each man. The ones watching Mike were happy to see that, on Saturday, he brought his whole family to the woodlot for the five children to play around and have fun. When lunchtime came, they were able to play further into the woods while Mom set the picnic up under a tree for shade, giving Mom and Dad time alone to sit and watch them play as they talked.

When Dad was ready to go back to work, he called the kids in for their lunch and told them that after lunch it was raspberry-picking time. He told them where it was and that it was the only place to pick, so they wouldn't get close to where he was working due to falling trees. Mom had buckets that looped on their belts for faster picking and took the two younger ones with a bucket of toys and a blanket to sit by the kids as they picked. It was nap time for the two little ones, so Mom could join the others picking after they fell asleep. The two oldest children grabbed the cooler and cups as they made their way to the patch.

They were all happy to pick, knowing a raspberry pie would be made for supper the next day and jam for toast in the winter—a little treat they appreciated during the colder months. The four oldest were very good pickers, and with Mom's help—and all the raspberries having never been picked yet—the gathering was fast and easy. The officers were happy to see how the family worked together as a unit.

The second set of officers assigned went to check out the maple shack Sam had talked about in court. They were checking to see how many furs were being dropped off, even with hunting season being over. They were surprised to see deer furs still being dropped off, and if there was more than one, they took the plate numbers to check them out. It was at that point they spotted a freezer where people were dropping off pieces of meat. Some meats were from stores—like hams and pork chops.

When dark came, they spotted Sam heading up the hill to the maple shack to collect what had been dropped off that day and take it back home. Sam had hidden cameras at the shack that were apparently well-hidden enough that the officers hadn't seen them yet—but Sam saw them clearly. They watched Sam all day long for days, only to see a man working on vehicles and full of grease.

Those watching Kevin found their days boring. Kevin was spending his time waiting for his unemployment check and going to town to get more supplies to work on his house. At night, it was rocking on his porch, drinking a few beers, and on occasion, someone would drop by and have one with him. At times, some of those people would show up and help him with his house. With the mill shut down, it gave many of them who stopped by something to do.

The officers had a meeting to discuss their findings. They realized it was time to check out the old man they had talked to and the farmer. They set up two wardens at each place, leaving the other two to do other work.

The ones assigned to the old man also had long days. The old man was clearly an old man, acting his age—slowly walking to his mailbox and clearly not able to do much of anything else. It took a whole week to clean up sticks that had fallen during the winter from his front yard. School kids came on Saturday to help clean the outside and bring his rocking chairs and table from the garage to the porch for summer. He always gave them an apple for helping him. The students were part of a senior help program from the high school.

His daughter came every Sunday with food for the week and cleaned up inside the house. Her daughters also came to make the job faster and visit with Grandpa before another week of school. They always had Sunday dinners together.

CHAPTER IX

Do They Have Their Man?

The wardens watching the farmer were very busy all the time trying not to be seen. He was a drinker with a lot of anger when he drank—mostly when the sun went down, but the drinking started way before that. During the day, he drank his own beer or what was left behind from the night before. People who visited him at night always brought beer over after milking time.

When you heard people say "he's himself now," that's when you knew he was toasted and complaining, and everything came out. There was no holding him back—anything and everything would come out, even stuff he shouldn't be saying. That was the time for officers to back off and go get a warrant to record conversations and return the next night.

The officers returned the next night and got as close as they could to catch it all. After the first night of this, the officers set it up so they could call in and not speak, allowing the office to record what was being said. The officers also had a tape recorder in hand so they could place it as close as possible, turn it on, and back off to not be seen in any way.

People who brought the beer over went for the entertainment of what they called story time. They knew he would be half gone by nightfall, so for less than a movie ticket, they could get him to that entertainment time. After beer four, they had the farmer in rare form. They told him his woodlot Vietnam man got off scot-free and clear. This is when the officers called in for the conversation to be recorded—going ever so close and quietly, only taking steps when laughter was loudest.

What came out clearly was:

"That murderer sells nothing but hollow trees to the mill, jipping them of money. Nothing but a murderer and a crook. They're stealing benefits from us War II vets who fought a real war. We didn't go around killing babies and kids—those cowards. They don't deserve our benefits, taking away from the real vets."

The officers slowly removed themselves from the scene, knowing they needed a bigger plan and more help to nail this guy they felt was their man. The one thing they talked about on their way to the office was the fact that the farmer said he sells nothing but hollow trees—and they felt that's how the warden may have gotten into the mill: by being placed in a hollow tree. And why not try to pin it on the Vietnam vet working the woodlot—who the farmer clearly seems to hate?

The picture is coming clear, but they need more to make sure it sticks.

At the officers' meeting, they still needed to connect how the murder occurred. Did the farmer think it was Mike on his property and thought he was shooting at him? Was it a hunting accident?

The first thing they did was check if the farmer had a hunting license—and they found he did. He also tagged a doe on opening day, which was before the officer went missing. So that pretty much counts him out on those grounds. And you can't arrest a person just for hating another.

The only clear thing they all seemed to agree on was that the body most likely ended up at the mill by being in a hollow log.

While looking to see if the farmer got his deer, they noticed a lot of deer were shot in that area. They decided to check those people out to see if anyone saw anything. They found nine hunters, some with juniors with them. They started by checking out their backgrounds. All seemed to be in good standing with the community, with no red flags showing up.

The officers started talking to each hunter, starting with those closest to the woodlot. The first two only started hunting after the warden was found to be missing for days and stayed on Sam's property only—not the woodlot. The third guy took his junior son out on Maine's opening day. They saw footprints in the light, powdered snow from the night before—footprints of a deer—and followed them to the woodlot. They saw no posted signs, so they continued to follow the tracks slowly and were ready if they ended up jumping a deer.

They came across a man more interested in writing on a paper than hunting. When the man spotted them, he dropped his paper (which he thought he was putting in his pocket) and took off out of the woods. The older hunter picked up the piece of paper and saw writings of logs cut and who picked up the load. The father told the son to save the paper and said they'd give it to the logger when they saw him.

As they told the officers this, the second officer asked him to describe the man. It clearly did not match Mike at all.

The officers asked if they could follow them to the woodlot and have them show where they were and where the guy was when they saw him. They agreed.

Mike happened to be working at the woodlot when the officers got there with the hunters. The officer asked the hunters if Mike was the man they saw.

They both said "NO" at the same time. Mike walked up to them asking what was going on. The officer explained they still hadn't caught who killed the warden and were checking all hunters in the area.

The hunter saw the look on his son's face. "Are you telling us this is not about a deer shooting?"

"Yes, sir," the officer answered. "These hunters saw a man watching you on this woodlot you're clearing, taking notes—but he had a gun on the ground next to his feet."

The hunter's son said, "I put one of those papers the man dropped on your windshield wipers of that truck over there."

Mike said, "That's my truck, and I did get that—and found it to be strange."

The officer asked Mike if he kept it.

Mike said, "Yes. I just put it in my truck glove compartment and felt at some point I would understand it."

"Can you get it for me while we go check the spot that guy was at?"

The officers and the hunters walked up to the spot in question. Snow season was gone, but you could clearly see someone was looking for something. The warden took pictures before anyone moved forward. The hunter's son stayed very close to his Dad.

They found a trail of coffee cups and soda cans, giving them a general idea of how the entry in that area was made. They bagged everything they found, like store receipts—hoping the stores have cameras. The hunter's son was so nervous he was looking hard for any little thing he could find. Then, caught between two trees that grew together until they branched out, was a bullet casing of a .30-30. The boy hollered to the warden, not touching it.

"Good job, son—that's the correct bullet casing we were looking for."

For a moment, the hunter looked toward the officers and stated, "Mike is logging from that mountaintop," and asked the officers, "Was the man looking to shoot that guy you called Mike? Makes you wonder if the warden jumped him to stop him and got shot instead. Looks like the result of a bidding war for the lot to me."

The officers took notice of what the hunter said for sure, but said, "Let's go see if the logger found that piece of paper." Sure enough, he did, but no name was on it. The officers asked if they saw any vehicle parked by the side of the road that day but were told they hadn't come in by those roads and were just following a deer. The officers thanked them for their help and were off to get what they had checked out.

CHAPTER X

Finally Have a Case

Now, having the casing and using the bullet from the mill's conveyor belt, ballistics were able to raise the percentage of possibility to 95%. Too much rain and snow were on the coffee cups to make a match of any kind, and there was not enough on the soda cans, which were facing down on the ground, for prints.

Now they needed to check out who wrote this note on the woodlot and why. They took a minute to think about the why. As the officers in the meeting brainstormed, one asked, "Why would anyone other than the logger keep track of logs going out? Maybe we should go see the person in charge of the bidding for this woodlot and find out what the bids were and how close they were on the bidding. It's a long shot, but we're six months into this and I know we're getting closer. We have no other clues and this seems real to me."

The wardens found out a logging company named D&B Logging not only finds the lots to clear out, but also does the logging to the mills themselves. They called ahead and were told to come right over. The manager made it clear to them that no one knows who else bid until the bidding is closed. "We run a fair company here. With two mills now closed, every dollar counts as we have the added cost of longer travel to some mills. No favoritism—we just take the lowest bid on getting the job done so we can make a profit on our end for subcontracting the job. The loggers have all been good to us and we treat them all by the same rule. It's all about the bucks like any other company. Only reliable workers are allowed to bid and even if they're off by a dollar, the lowest bid wins."

"The top two lowest bids were only $200 apart. Mike got the job and I must say he is getting more log boards out of that lot than we expected, which is more bucks for us as a company." The officers asked for a list of those who bid on the lot, starting with the lowest bid. They already knew what was going on from the papers and had the list ready and handed it to them. "You'll see the addresses are all there for you."

The officers got back to the office and pulled pictures from their driver's licenses to show the father and son to see if the man they saw was one of them. The son identified the man, who was the second-lowest bidder, right away. George lost the bid by $200. The officers went to see the judge to get a warrant to search George's house.

As soon as they found the .30-30, they placed George under arrest and took him in. George said he was only keeping track of how many loads were being taken out, only to see how many logs the area had. The officers asked, "Why spend six months doing that instead of looking for another woodlot to cut?" George did not answer. His explanation for having the gun was that it was hunting season, but the warden knew this did not add up as George had already gotten his deer at the time the father and son saw him with a gun by his side.

Mike had taken less than usual in the bid because he had walked the lot to check what would be red oak board footage and what would end up as hardwood pulpwood—two needs of the mill from this woodlot.

So the wardens had the motive of losing the lot over $200, the opportunity of witnesses seeing him at the lot and running when spotted, and leaving evidence behind in his own writing. This meant, of course, his gun and the bullet matched almost 100%. George got 25 years in prison and did not seem upset over it. This left the officers thinking the story was much bigger than that. The warden may not have been the intended target but was in the wrong place at the wrong time—all over two hundred bucks.

CHAPTER XI

Finding Their Way

Mike was about finished at the woodlot by the time the court case was over. Kevin was still lost but collecting his unemployment check. Sam's garage was just too small for any big jobs that paid more. One night, Mike called his lifelong friends to come over for a meeting.

"How about we've had enough of this outside work? Sam, you seem to have a good line of clients working in your small garage, and look at the community support you've gotten after being arrested. So, you're used to the people connection thing after the war. How about the 'A' team goes back to our plans of owning our own business? This way, you can work with more space, and we can get a service tech to write the orders and deal with customers to take that weight off you."

"How does that sound to you?"

"I'd love it, Mike. You always were the brain to make things happen. I'm glad you thought of the people dealings for me."

"Kevin, you still good with organizing?"

"Yes, for sure, you've seen my house." "You hire salespeople so you don't have to deal with the people directly until you feel ready. Train them to do the talking your way for that professional, organized way to make the sale. You watch what your salespeople do and how they treat the customers. I will oversee the contracts and find the best loan officer for them according to their credit score and the payments they can afford. Are you all in?"

"YES," was said all together.

Mike says, "I'll deal with the bank."

Sam, look for a big parking lot and showroom. Check out how many bays so you know how many mechanics you'll need, but leave one bay always open for drive-ins. No mechanic for that bay until we're on our feet and rolling well.

"Kevin will start with three salespeople, and if you find one that's good and is a lady, we hire them too here. Did you keep the paperwork from before?"

"Yes, I did, but the address will be different."

"Does anyone know if the old spot was taken or could be retaken?"

Sam says, "I think a bakery took it because I remember smelling fresh baked bread in the air every early morning."

"Come to think of it, I haven't smelled that for a few months now. I'll check that out first."

"Okay, let's meet again at the end of the week and see where we're all."

A week has passed, and they all meet at Mike's house again. Sam reports first with good news.

"The place we first found in high school is back up for sale. The bakery just went under three months ago. It's now up for ten thousand less than before, probably due to work needed. We can do the work, I'm sure. So, we have a meeting with them tomorrow to see the inside and check how much of the place has changed and what will be needed to bring it back to our needs. From what I could see from the windows, the bays don't look like they were touched, but the showroom floor will need restructuring and a new floor. Some offices were removed for a bigger front room, so we will have to see what has been left and what we will need when we see it. However, it would save us from having to reorder paperwork. That was a big expense back in our high school days. I'll get it all down from the attic and see how it has held up over the years. I did check with the high school on those graduating in the mechanic skills and have seven applications for us to review. I only took those who were good-natured and strong workers. Their schoolwork was always done on time and well, with teacher recommendations."

"Kevin, how are your salespeople coming?"

"Well, I found two from a debate team. I gave them some of our old brochures of cars to read up on for their second interview. They need to know the vehicles well in order to sell them, and they both have some vehicle repair background that can work to our benefit. I do need to find one more and hope Sam can take part with me in that second interview. The more they know, the better our sales will be. Great job, Kevin!"

"Well, now for my part. I met with two banks willing to take us on as a new business. Now, as for us all being equal partners, we have to sign only for this business, not anyone's home. Let me make that clear. This is a military business loan to start a new business, and we're all vets, so the interest rate is as low as they come. With ten thousand lower in the cost of the place and military low interest, we make out better than we ever could imagine. Let's make opening day right after graduation for those we hired and bring our dream plan back."

"The 'A' team is back to living our dream. Now Sam, aren't you happy the 'A' team got together to bail you out of that one?"

THE END!

Some of My Other Books on Amazon:

1. Blind Affection

2. 3rd Floor

3. Gigolo of the Country Park

4. Toxic Fall

5. Paws of Fate

6. Broken Hearts & Souls

7. Splash of Love

8. Life of an Old Woodsman

9. The Torment's of the Modest Secluded Farm Life

10. Easy & Inexpensive Holiday Classroom Crafts for Teachers

ABOUT THE AUTHOR

In 1981, she became a certified community advocate, dedicated to helping her community. She started as a Tiny Todd group leader, raising funds to benefit low-income children and supporting families in areas where she was trained.

In 1984, she received a certificate for her volunteer service from the University of Maine Cooperative Extension. Her work focused on teaching children to cook and promoting proper nutritional values.

She then served as treasurer for the Task Force on Human Needs and became a member of its board of directors. Additionally, she was Vice President of the

Maine Association of Independent Neighborhoods, working on legislation to support the community. She also served as Vice President of the American Legion Auxiliary in Lisbon Falls, helping veterans and raising funds.

For many years, she volunteered in schools, earning several awards. Starting with Head Start and continuing through three different schools, she contributed by making costumes for plays, publishing children's personal classroom books, coordinating weekly fluoride treatments for an entire school, and organizing her favorite classroom crafts. These crafts were often holiday-themed or related to weekly lessons, designed to help students retain what they learned.

Now, at the age of 70, she brings stories to life.

* 9 7 8 1 9 6 8 6 1 5 7 7 2 *